DISNEY

THE
JUNGLE BOOK

Deep in the jungle, Bagheera the panther was out hunting. Suddenly, he heard a strange crying sound coming from the river. He discovered a baby tucked inside a basket.

"Why, it's a Man-cub!" he thought. "This little chap needs food and a mother's care. Perhaps Mother Wolf will look after him."

Mother Wolf agreed to help. They
named the Man-cub Mowgli, and he
grew up safe and happy in the jungle.

Mowgli loved being a wolf pup. But everything changed when Mowgli was ten years old. Shere Khan, the man-eating tiger, heard about the Man-cub and came searching for him.

The wolves held an urgent meeting to discuss Mowgli's future. They agreed that Bagheera should take the boy to the Man-village where he would be safe.

The next morning, Bagheera and Mowgli set off on their long journey. Mowgli was angry and upset. He didn't understand why he had to leave the jungle. It was his home!

When darkness fell, Bagheera and Mowgli settled down to sleep in a tree. Nearby, Kaa, the snake, was hiding in some leaves. Kaa slithered toward the Man-cub.

Kaa's shining yellow eyes seemed to have a magic power on Mowgli. The boy sank into a deep trance.

Kaa slowly wound himself around Mowgli, ready to swallow him up!

Suddenly, Bagheera woke up and sprang at Kaa. He gave the snake a terrible blow and sent him slithering away into the jungle.

At dawn, Mowgli sneaked away. Bagheera found him, but Mowgli refused to go to the Man-village. This made Bagheera so cross, he left. The Man-cub was all alone.

But not for long! Mowgli met a friendly bear named Baloo.

"Well, now, what have we here?" Baloo asked.

Mowgli introduced himself. He told Baloo he wanted to stay in the jungle.

"No problem, Little Britches," said Baloo. "I'll look after you!"

Baloo enjoyed teaching his new friend about the "bear necessities" of life. Soon Mowgli could fight like a bear, growl like a bear, and even scratch like a bear!

Later that afternoon, Mowgli and
Baloo waded into the river to keep cool.
As they floated along, Mowgli sat on the
big bear's tummy, and Baloo fell asleep.

Monkeys were watching from the
trees, waiting to kidnap the Man-cub.
They swung down and grabbed him!

"Hey! Let go of me!" Mowgli cried.

Baloo woke with a jump . . .

. . . but it was too late! The monkeys were
carrying Mowgli off to the ruined temple
where they lived. Luckily, Bagheera heard
Mowgli's cries. He found Baloo, who
explained what had happened, and the two
made a plan to rescue Mowgli.

At the ruined temple, Louie, King of the Apes, was sitting on his throne, waiting for the Man-cub. He offered to help Mowgli stay in the jungle. In return, he wanted the secret of Man's red fire.

"Once I am the master of fire," Louie said, " I will be human just like you!"

King Louie declared a great feast and dance in honor of Mowgli.

Mowgli's feet tapped to the music and he joined the fun— just as Baloo and Bagheera reached the temple.

King Louie noticed a beautiful lady
ape. He rushed over to ask her to dance.
But as the "lady ape" danced . . .

. . . his disguise
began to fall off!
It was Baloo!
The monkeys had
been tricked, and
Bagheera had
grabbed Mowgli!

What a ruckus there was! The monkeys attacked Baloo. Bagheera rushed over to help, and Baloo knocked down part of the temple. In all the confusion, they were able to drag Mowgli to safety deep within the jungle.

That night, while the Man-cub slept, Baloo and Bagheera discussed his future.

"The Man-cub *must* go back to the Man-village," Bagheera insisted. "The jungle is not the place for him."

But the next day, Mowgli ran off again!
"The Man-cub is alone in the jungle,"
said Bagheera. "We must find him before
Shere Khan does."

He did not
know that Shere
Khan was close
by . . . listening.

Shere Khan caught Mowgli's scent.
He spotted him and snarled. The tiger
leaped at him with claws bared—and
then jolted to a stop!

Baloo had caught him by the tail!

Shere Khan roared with rage and
flipped Baloo over his head. The bear
hit the ground with a great thud.

Suddenly, lightning
struck and a tree burst
into flames. Shere Khan
was terrified of fire!

Mowgli grabbed a
burning branch and tied
it to the tiger's tail.
Shere Khan screamed
and fled into the jungle,
never to be seen again.

Mowgli ran over to the fallen bear and cried, "Baloo, get up! Oh, no! Baloo!"

Was Baloo dead?

No! The big bear sat up and rubbed his eyes. Mowgli laughed and threw his arms round his friend's neck.

A short time later, the three friends
saw the Man-village on the other side
of the river . . . and they heard someone
singing. There at the river's edge was a
young girl fetching water. This made
Mowgli curious.

"I've never seen one before!" he said.

The girl turned and smiled. Mowgli
shyly smiled back.

Baloo and Bagheera watched as Mowgli picked up the girl's water jug and followed her. Just before Mowgli walked through the entrance to the village, he turned to smile at his old friends.

"Mowgli is where he belongs," sighed Bagheera.

"Come on," said Baloo. "Let's get back to where *we* belong."